Gulliver's Adventures in Lilliput

from *Gulliver's Travels* by Jonathan Swift
retold by Jenny Alexander

Jonathan Swift was nearly sixty when he
wrote Gulliver's Travels in 1726. He was a
clergyman, but he had worked for the
government in his youth.

The book is set in four imaginary countries.
Swift pokes fun at the people who run
them, as a way of criticising the real-life
government of his day.

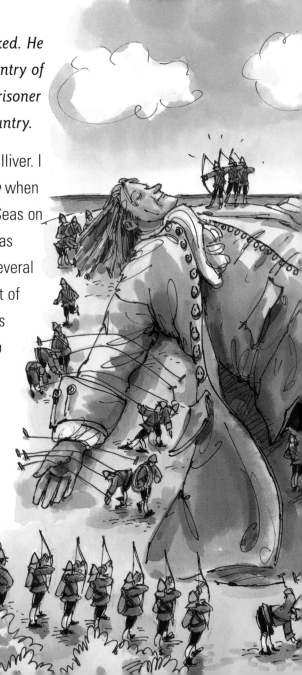

Chapter 1

The author is shipwrecked. He comes ashore in the country of Lilliput. He is made a prisoner and carried up the country.

My name is Lemuel Gulliver. I was on the *Antelope* when she set sail for the South Seas on May 4th, 1699. The ship was wrecked in a storm after several months at sea, and the rest of the crew were drowned. As night fell, I was washed up onto a lonely beach. I walked a little way, then lay down and went to sleep. When I woke up it was daylight.

I tried to get up, but I couldn't move. Suddenly, I felt something climb onto my left leg and walk up my body to my chin. It was a tiny human being! Before I could get over the shock of seeing him, lots more ran up my leg and across my body. One of them cried in a small clear voice, "Hekinah Degul!", and they all joined in.

3

I struggled and my left arm came free. The creatures ran away. One of them shouted "Togo Phonac!", and they shot arrows at me. Some stuck into my left hand like needles. Others stuck into my body and face. I tried to get up again, but they shot more arrows at me. I stopped struggling.

They built a platform about one and a half feet high. One of the creatures climbed up to the top where I could see him and made a speech. I couldn't understand a word he said. When he had finished, I put my left hand to my mouth, to show I was hungry.

About a hundred of the creatures climbed up onto my chest, carrying baskets of bread and meat. Each leg of mutton or beef was the size of a lark's wing, and the loaves were no bigger than bullets.

They brought me two barrels of wine, which held about half a pint each. I could have grabbed some of the creatures, but I didn't want them to shoot any more arrows at me. They removed the arrows that were still stuck into my skin, and rubbed some ointment into my wounds. Then I fell into a deep sleep, because the wine had been drugged.

While I was asleep, they untied me. They lifted me onto a cart and took me to the capital city. We stopped outside the gates, by an old temple. It had a doorway about four feet high and two feet wide, with a small window on each side. Through the left one, they put ninety-one chains, which they attached to my left leg with thirty-six padlocks. Then they undid the strings that tied me onto the cart.

I stood up. The people were amazed how tall I was. The chains were about two yards long, so I could hardly walk. I crawled inside the temple and lay down on the floor. I had never felt so unhappy in my life.

Chapter 2

The Emperor pays a visit. The author shows he can be gentle. His pockets are searched and his sword and pistols taken away.

The next morning, the Emperor came to see me. He had his sword in his hand, in case I attacked him. We took turns to speak, although neither of us could understand what the other one said.

After he had gone, a crowd gathered round, and some shot arrows at me. The soldiers rounded up six of them, tied them up, and handed them over to me. I put five in my pocket, and held the other one up to my face. I took out my knife. The crowd gasped. But then I cut his bonds and put him down. I did the same thing with each of the others.

Meanwhile, the Emperor was talking to his Ministers. What if I escaped? What if I cost them so much in food that the country went bankrupt? What if I caused a famine? Now they had got me, they didn't know what to do with me.

When the Emperor heard how I had treated my prisoners, he decided to be kind to me. He sent six hundred servants to look after me, and six teachers to teach me the language. He also sent two servants to search my pockets. They made a list of everything they found.

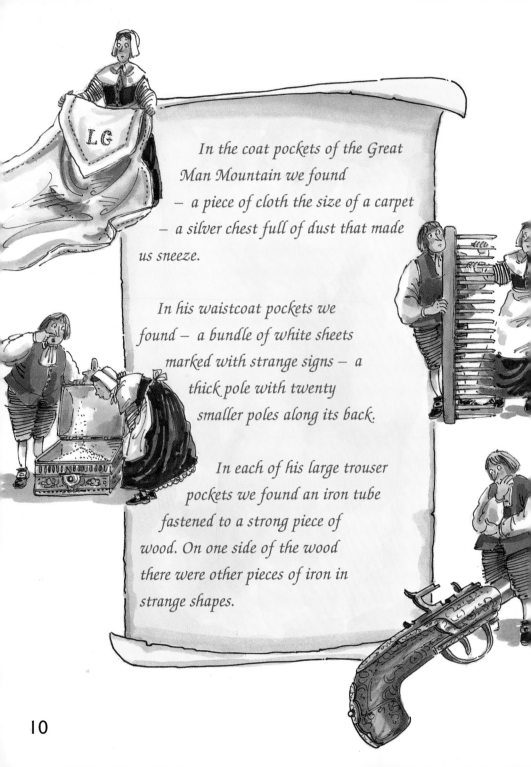

In the coat pockets of the Great
Man Mountain we found
— a piece of cloth the size of a carpet
— a silver chest full of dust that made
us sneeze.

In his waistcoat pockets we
found — a bundle of white sheets
marked with strange signs — a
thick pole with twenty
smaller poles along its back.

In each of his large trouser
pockets we found an iron tube
fastened to a strong piece of
wood. On one side of the wood
there were other pieces of iron in
strange shapes.

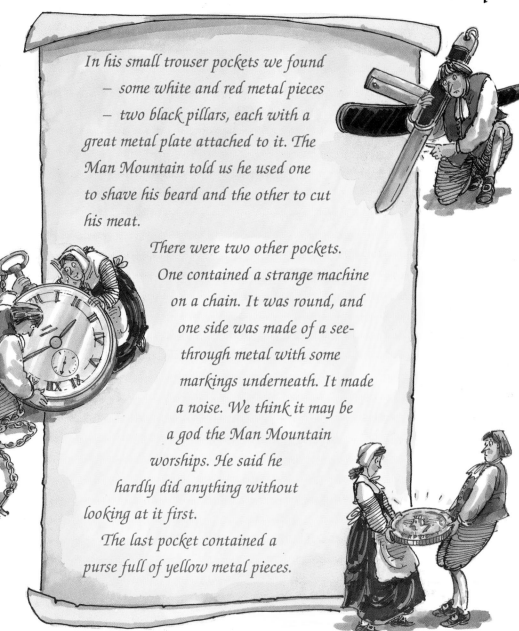

In his small trouser pockets we found
— some white and red metal pieces
— two black pillars, each with a
great metal plate attached to it. The
Man Mountain told us he used one
to shave his beard and the other to cut
his meat.

There were two other pockets.
One contained a strange machine
on a chain. It was round, and
one side was made of a see-
through metal with some
markings underneath. It made
a noise. We think it may be
a god the Man Mountain
worships. He said he
hardly did anything without
looking at it first.
The last pocket contained a
purse full of yellow metal pieces.

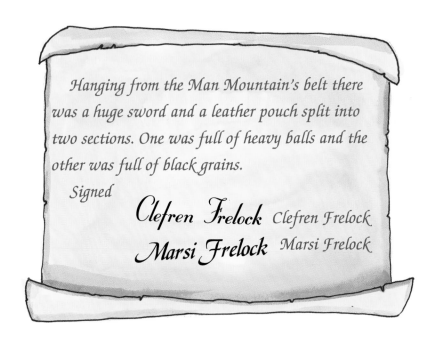

*Hanging from the Man Mountain's belt there
was a huge sword and a leather pouch split into
two sections. One was full of heavy balls and the
other was full of black grains.*

Signed

Clefren Frelock Clefren Frelock

Marsi Frelock Marsi Frelock

The Emperor wanted to see one of my hollow iron tubes, by which he meant my pistols. I put some powder in one, but no ball, and fired it. Half the people fell over in fright.

I handed over both pistols, my powder and bullets, my sword, my silver and copper money, my purse full of gold, my knife and razor, comb, silver snuff box, handkerchief and journal.

But I didn't let them find my glasses.
I wanted to keep them safe.

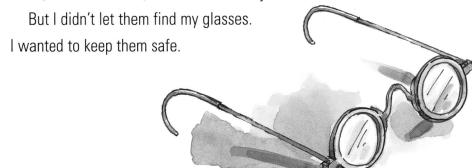

Chapter 3

The author is allowed his freedom.

The Emperor showed me how he chose his government. Ministers had to dance on a rope about two feet above the ground, and the ones who jumped the highest without falling off got the best jobs.

When the Emperor wanted to hand out some honours, he and the First Minister would hold a long stick parallel to the ground and people would jump over it or creep under it. The person who could creep the lowest and leap the highest got a red thread. The second-best got a blue one, and the third best got a green one. I have never seen anything like it in all the courts of Europe.

After a while, the Emperor told his ministers that he wanted to set me free. Skyresh Bolgolam said I should have to make some promises first. He wrote the list himself.

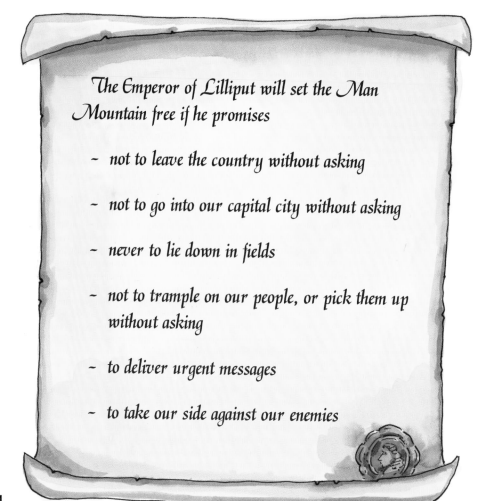

The Emperor of Lilliput will set the Man Mountain free if he promises

- not to leave the country without asking

- not to go into our capital city without asking

- never to lie down in fields

- not to trample on our people, or pick them up without asking

- to deliver urgent messages

- to take our side against our enemies

I had to make my promise in the Lilliput way, by holding my right foot in my left hand and placing the middle finger of my right hand on the top of my head and the thumb on the tip of my right ear.

Chapter 4

The author visits Mildendo, the capital city.
He offers to help the Emperor in his wars.

As soon as I was free, I asked if I could visit the capital city, Mildendo. The people were told to stay off the streets.

There was a wall around the city about two and a half feet high and eleven inches wide. It was an exact square, each side being five hundred feet long. Two broad streets, about five feet wide, divided it into quarters. All the other lanes and alleys were too narrow for me to walk in. The buildings were between three and five storeys high.

The palace stood in the centre. When I bent down to look inside, the Empress held out her hand for me to kiss.

About a fortnight later Reldresal, the Principal Secretary for Private Affairs, came to see me. He told me that Lilliput was not as peaceful as it seemed. It was at war with the Island of Blefuscu, which they believed to be the only other country in the world. They thought I had just dropped out of the sky.

The war started like this. Long ago, everyone agreed that you should eat a boiled egg from the larger end. But the Emperor's grandfather, when he was a boy, cut his finger opening his egg at the larger end. So his father, who was Emperor at that time, passed a law that everyone should open their eggs at the smaller end from then on.

The people didn't like the new law. Eleven thousand had been killed for refusing to open their eggs at the smaller end. Many books had been written on the subject, but those of the Big-Endians were banned. Big-Endians were not allowed to work.

Some Big-Endians ran away, and the King of Blefuscu took them in. He said the Lilliput law went against the teachings of the great prophet, Lustrog, who said, "All true believers shall break their eggs at the best end." Now the King of Blefuscu had built a new fleet of ships, and was getting ready to attack. The Emperor had sent Reldresal to ask for my help.

I said that being a foreigner I couldn't really understand the argument, but that I would certainly defend Lilliput against any attack.

21

Chapter 5

The author prevents an attack. Visitors come from Blefuscu. The author saves the palace from burning down.

The sea between Lilliput and Blefuscu was eight hundred yards across and no more than six feet deep. I worked out a way to seize the enemy fleet and bring it back to Lilliput.

I made fifty strong hooks from iron bars, and tied them to thick ropes. Then I waded across the sea to Blefuscu.

When the people in the ships saw me coming, they dived into the water and swam for their lives.

I fixed one hook to the front of each ship and knotted the ropes together. The Blefuscu people shot arrows at me as I worked, and I was worried about my eyes. Then I remembered my glasses.

I towed the ships back to Lilliput. The Emperor was waiting for me
on the beach. He asked me to help him take over Blefuscu. Then the
whole world would have to open their eggs at the smaller end! But I
told him I would not help to turn free people into slaves.

About three weeks later, the King of Blefuscu sent six of his Ministers to ask for peace. When they heard I had refused to help the Emperor destroy them, they invited me to visit their country. I asked the Emperor. He took it as a sign that I wanted to change sides. So I was glad when I got a chance - or so I thought - to get in the Emperor's good books again.

It happened like this. In the middle of the night, a fire broke out in the royal palace. As luck would have it, I had drunk a lot of wine that evening.

I ran to the palace, and did something no-one else could do for me. The fire was soon put out.

I went straight home without waiting to be thanked. I felt sure the Emperor would be pleased with me for saving the palace, but I could see he might not like the way I had done it.

Chapter 6

The author is warned of a plot against him.

Not long after, a friend came to warn me that a plot that had been hatched against me. Flimnap, the Treasurer, and Skyresh Bolgolam, the High Admiral, had accused me of treason. My friend showed me a copy of the case against me.

The Case against Quinbus Flestrin
(the Man Mountain)

1   Quinbus Flestrin has broken the
    law against passing water
    inside the palace grounds.

2   He has refused to help our
    Emperor defeat Blefuscu,
    although the only excuse he can
    come up with is that he doesn't
    want to destroy the lives of
    innocent people.

My enemies had already thought of three ways of putting me to death: they could set fire to my house when I was asleep, shoot me with poisoned arrows, or soak my clothes in poison and let it seep into my skin.

But my good friend Reldresal asked the Emperor to spare my life. He suggested they just put my eyes out instead. He said people liked a leader who was merciful and besides, I might still be of use. Being blind could make me more fearless, as the only thing I was worried about when I took the enemy's fleet was getting an arrow in my eye. Besides, I didn't need to be able to see things for myself because I could just let the Ministers tell me what was going on, the way great rulers do.

But Skyresh Bolgolam and Flimnap said I was a traitor, and traitors had to die.

The Emperor liked the idea of blinding me, but agreed that it wouldn't be much of a punishment. So my friend, Reldresal, suggested that after they had blinded me they might give me less and less to eat, so that I would fade away and die.

They decided to tell me I was to be blinded for my crimes. As I was getting off so lightly, they expected me to be grateful and agree to the punishment. They weren't planning to say anything about starving me afterwards.

Being an ordinary person and knowing nothing about courts and justice, I must confess the sentence seemed a bit harsh to me. So I made a decision which, although it saved my sight and freedom, was probably wrong. I went to Blefuscu.

Chapter 7

*The author finds the means to leave
Blefuscu and return home.*

Three days after I arrived in Blefuscu, I was walking on the shore when I saw a boat floating upside-down in the sea. Having brought it ashore, I found that it was hardly damaged at all. The King of Blefuscu said I could leave if I wanted to.

When I was ready to go, the King gave me some money and a picture of himself. He also gave me food and drink for my voyage, as well as some live cattle and sheep. I wanted to take some people too, but the King would not allow it.

After two days at sea, I saw a ship. The Captain took me on board. At first, he didn't believe me when I told him about my adventures, so I showed him my animals.

When we got back to England, I made a lot of money showing my cows and sheep to people. But life seemed dull after such an adventure, and I soon decided to set off again.

Scotstown Primary School
Scotstown Road
Bridge of Don
Aberdeen
AB22 8HH

Tel: 01224 703331

Other titles in the Independent Plus Stage

Classic Texts
Dr Jekyll and Mr Hyde
Gulliver's Adventures in Lilliput

Plays
Magical Scenes from Shakespeare's A Midsummer Night's Dream
Supernatural Scenes from Shakespeare's Macbeth

Poetry
The Lady of Shalott
The Song of Hiawatha

•Visit *www.literacyland.co.uk*
for free activities and fun games!

Genre Range access

Independent Plus Stage

Gulliver's
Adventures in Lilliput

Travel with Gulliver on his unforgettable
voyage and follow his adventures in the
strange land of Lilliput.

Literacy Land

PEARSON Education

Genre Range is part of Literacy Land
www.literacyland.co.uk

ISBN 0-582-77035

9 780582 770355